Nature Fights Back

Contents

Written by Simon Chapman

Collins

Introduction

Around the world, wild nature is in crisis. Forests are being cut down. Oceans are being polluted. The climate is changing. And nearly all of this is the fault of the human race.

But **extinctions** of animals and plants are nothing new. Life has existed on Earth for 4,000 million years and several times natural disasters have killed nearly all of it. The most recent of these "**extinction events**" was 66 million years ago when a comet impact wiped out the dinosaurs and many other whole animal families.

Afterwards, Earth recovered. Over time, new **species** evolved and around 200,000 years ago, *homo sapiens* (humans, like us) came to exist. Humans started affecting other life on the planet by hunting and farming. This has been going on for the past 10,000 years – since the end of the last ice age. This is a blink of an eye in the history of life on Earth.

But the human race does not have to cause the next extinction event. When nature is left alone, species come back to damaged **habitats**; this is called **"rewilding".** In 2020, during the coronavirus lockdowns when there was less traffic and less pollution, wildlife moved into urban spaces. Meadow flowers grew up on roadside verges that were left uncut and bees arrived to pollinate them. Across the world, people saw (and often filmed) animals walking along their city streets, from deer in Japan and elephants in India to jackass penguins in Cape Town, South Africa.

No species has ever had the power to change nature as much as our own, and we can change things for the better. We can conserve resources and produce less pollution. We can preserve natural habitats and help other areas go back to nature. We can help nature fight back.

1 Rewilding damaged habitats

The DMZ minefields and watchtowers – nature returns to a war zone

Picture the scene: a strip of land, four kilometres wide, that runs west to east for 250 kilometres over rugged mountains from one coast to another. Both sides of the strip are edged with high barbed wire fences. There are watchtowers with machine guns and bunkers full of armed troops every few hundred metres. The land between the two armies is peppered with landmines and covered by heavy guns hidden in the countryside behind. No one goes in here anymore. To enter means death.

This is the DMZ ("Dee-Em-Zee"), the so-called Demilitarised Zone between the borders of North Korea and South Korea in East Asia. The two countries went to war in 1950 and, when that war ended, it was agreed that there should be some land between them which nobody was allowed to enter. Since then, that narrow band has been left alone. No one has built roads over it or farmed it.

It has gone wild. Forests have grown and wetlands have flooded as vegetation has clogged waterways. In the sea to either side of the Korean peninsula, marine habitats have thrived. The whole area has become an accidental wildlife paradise.

North Korea

Pyongyang

Seoul

South Korea

white-naped cranes

Amur leopard

Most obvious of the new residents are long-legged birds called cranes. These use the new marshes as winter stopovers to feed on insects, frogs and plant roots during their yearly journey from north-eastern China and Mongolia. The 1.3 metre-tall white-naped crane is the most abundant kind. There are also increasing numbers of the bigger and ultra-rare red-crowned crane. In Korean culture, cranes represent good fortune and long life. The red-crowned crane was nearing extinction until new areas of habitat opened up for it in the DMZ.

long-tailed goral

The coast on either side of the border zone is also rewilding. With no one fishing the waters (any fishing boats would be sunk), the sea here is a haven for many types of marine life, including 12-metre-long grey whales which until recently had rarely been seen off the Korean coast.

The **temperate** forest, which has grown over what used to be farmland and open country, is thriving too. There are now healthy populations of lynx, Asiatic black bears and a rare type of goat-antelope called the long-tailed goral. There have been rumours of sightings of the endangered Amur leopard, and possibly even Siberian tigers.

9

Rewilding Chernobyl – how a deserted city turned into wilderness

Ukraine. 26 April 1986. A steam explosion blows the Chernobyl **nuclear power station** apart, blanketing the area with a cloud of debris and water vapour which gives out harmful radiation (this can damage living things and cause cancer). Some of the **contamination** reaches as far as Scotland over 2,000 kilometres away. All the people from the nearby town of Pripyat and its surroundings are evacuated from the danger zone. Even so, over the following years, thousands of people contract cancer and there is an unusually high number of birth defects.

Scientists say the area around the reactor will remain dangerous for 20,000 years. The danger zone is fenced off and left alone.

And over time, nature returns.

Even though radiation levels are dangerously high in Pripyat, a forest springs up amongst the derelict blocks of flats, and wildlife moves in. Many of the birch and pine trees have now grown to over 20 metres tall, level with the tops of the buildings. There are even saplings growing on their flat roofs. Elks, European bison and brown bears, which always lived in the surrounding countryside, have moved into the deserted city. So have Przewalski's wild horses. Common in caveman times, these horses were wiped out from virtually all of Europe and Asia until, by the 1960s, there was just one wild herd left in Mongolia. Thirty-one Przewalski's horses were introduced to Chernobyl's exclusion zone in 1998 in a study to see how the original wildlife of the area would fare without humans around. They are breeding successfully despite the radiation.

How did everything come back?

Ecological succession is the name for how **ecosystems** change over time – in this case, how nature came back after the Chernobyl disaster.

Wind-blown seeds of hardy plants like silver birch began to grow in cracks in the concrete and tarmac. Their roots pushed down, forcing the cracks wider. The young trees grew upwards, filling the light gaps. Herbivores – plant eaters like hares, red squirrels and roe deer – fed on the plants. Their dung nourished the new soil and brought in more seeds, like acorns which grew into oak trees.

Predators came in to hunt the herbivores. Some, like foxes, were already living in the city. Lynxes and wolves moved in from nearby forests. With lots of prey and no people to hunt them, they thrived. There are now seven times more wolves in Chernobyl than in the surrounding area.

As with the humans who live nearby, the wildlife in the exclusion zone also suffers from the high radiation levels. The cancer rate amongst the animals that live around Chernobyl is high, but some animals survive. Having suitable habitats and no humans hunting them means that far more live to breed than die of radiation poisoning and cancer.

But there are still problems. Some areas close to the blast site were so badly contaminated by radioactive substances that the forest there died. People called it the "Red Forest" as the pine needles turned rust-coloured, and they sent bulldozers to bury the trees. Then the insects, fungi and microscopic soil life that rot the dead wood were nearly wiped out. Nearly, but not quite. The contamination will stay in the soil for years but with luck, the tiny creatures which recycle **nutrients** back into the soil will bounce back.

In under 50 years, Chernobyl has become one of the most wildlife-rich habitats in Europe and really shows how hardy nature is, even when faced with potentially lethal amounts of radiation.

Lost cities in the jungle

The DMZ reverted into wilderness in only 50 years. At Chernobyl, a town is now engulfed in forest after little more than 30 years. With more time, whole cities can be "swallowed up", especially in the tropical rainforests where continual warmth and moisture means plants grow much quicker. "Lost cities" in the jungle do exist. And they are still being discovered.

One of the most famous lost cities is Tikal in the Peten region of Guatemala, Central America. It was built by the ancient Mayan people who deserted it – no one knows why – around 950 CE. In the time since then, the rainforest grew back. Trees and liana creepers grew over the buildings and stepped pyramids where the Mayans used to worship. The seeds of the incoming plants were brought in by the wind and in the droppings of animals and birds. In time, rotting vegetation became soil, and this nourished more plants which grew on top. Gradually, the rainforest grew back. The trees grew huge, their roots growing into cracks in the stonework, splitting it and making more soil. Now, after more than a thousand years, the rainforest growing over the deserted city looks just like the jungle surrounding it, though scientific analysis has shown there are still not quite as many types of plant.

Tikal was "discovered" by European explorers in the 19th century. Since then, the vegetation has been cut away from the main pyramids so that tourists can see what they once looked like. But the city is vast and most of it is still untouched, home to spider monkeys, toucans, jaguars and much more besides.

Did you know?

Tikal is just one of many lost cities that have been smothered by the Central American rainforest. A combination of lasers and ground-mapping radar (LiDAR) mounted in aircraft has found others that are 1,000 years older. LiDAR has also shown that some of the biggest hills in the Peten are actually pyramids even taller than the 60-metre ones uncovered at Tikal.

The sunken fleet of Chuuk Lagoon

There are lost cities and other man-made structures reclaimed by nature in different habitats across the world, including under the sea. One such place where life returned after being almost wiped out is the Chuuk Lagoon in the Caroline Islands of the Pacific Ocean.

Chuuk was the site of a naval battle in the Second World War. Forty ships were sunk, including three tankers which leaked their cargoes of diesel and gasoline into the water. Despite the oil spills, toxic chemicals and blasting with high explosives, the wildlife came back.

Shipwrecks litter the seafloor, along with their cargoes of tanks, torpedoes, lorries and railway carriages. The wrecks are now covered in coral and home to vast numbers of fish and other marine life. Chuuk Lagoon is fringed with a barrier reef that protects it from the buffeting of the ocean waves, leaving the water inside calm, clear and sunlit, the perfect place for coral to grow. Though it spends most of its life fixed in one place, coral is actually an animal. Young coral (larvae) look like miniature jellyfish. They float in the sea currents and when they make contact with rocks – and shipwrecks – they cling on. This is what happened at Chuuk.

Once fixed, the coral **polyps** build stony casings around themselves for protection. They also bring in simple **algae** plants which use sunlight to produce food by photosynthesis. In turn, the coral uses this food for growth and movement. At night, the polyps feed by sending out tentacles into the water to grab tiny animals as they drift past. Over the years, the corals' rocky outsides join together and a stony "forest" called a reef builds up.

Coral reefs have been called the "rainforests of the seas". They form the habitat for thousands of sea creatures. Some feed on the coral polyps or use the reef for shelter. Others are predators that eat the coral-feeders. The combination of living things interacting together in their habitat is called an ecosystem and coral reef ecosystems are amongst the richest on the planet.

Marine life at Chuuk Lagoon returned because there were other coral reefs nearby. The coral-encrusted fleet has become one of the world's foremost scuba diving sites. Surgeonfish and angelfish are particularly numerous, but there are also dolphins, eagle rays and various types of shark such as blacktip reef sharks and hammerhead sharks. The wrecks don't have as many species as nearby lagoons – yet – but they will do in time.

angelfish

blue tang or surgeonfish

blacktip reef shark

Urban wildlife – cities gone wild

If you look around the place where you live, you'll see nature trying to take over. Soil builds up at the edges of buildings. Dust builds up inside your house or flat. Weeds grow into the cracks in pavements and up walls.

Take another look at that area of waste ground along a disused railway line, alongside a city canal or even in your own backyard – anywhere that's been left to go wild for a few months. You might be surprised by what you see.

Flocks of goldfinches feed on the seedheads of
the weeds that spring up, and sparrowhawks swoop
out from the cover of bushes to hunt them. There are
dragonflies wherever there is open water, and there
are butterflies. Stinging nettles are fantastic food for all
sorts of caterpillars. So are brambles. In early autumn,
their fruit – blackberries – is eaten by thrushes, voles
and beetles, and moths use their long tongues to lick up
the sugary juice. The moths, in turn, are prey to foraging
birds like blackcaps and long-tailed tits.

Urban wildlife is often right under our noses, either unseen or ignored. With more people and fewer natural habitats, many wild animals and plants are finding places to live in our cities. Foxes picking through rubbish or hunting in gardens and areas of waste ground are common all over Europe. In North America, coyotes also do this. So do black bears. In Mumbai in India, they even have urban leopards. Most people don't realise they are living so close by, as the big cats are nocturnal and so remain unseen as they stalk the parks and alleyways, hunting for stray dogs under the cover of darkness.

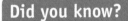

Did you know?

In Alaska, moose are regular visitors to the streets at the edges of towns. So are racoons, all across North America, which will raid dustbins to eat any food waste they find. Macaque monkeys in Thailand, Sri Lanka and India are also quite happy to eat food that people leave behind. In many places, they live around Hindu or Buddhist temples and the worshippers keep them better fed than they would be in their original jungle homes.

Saltwater crocodiles sometimes live in the drains in the towns of Australia's Northern Territories. People often only discover they are there when flood water from storms flushes them out.

In Sauraha in Nepal, there is even an urban rhino. A large male Indian one-horned rhino wanders through the streets every evening on its way from the tall grass and jungle on one side of town to similar habitat on the other side. People built the town over the rhinos' age-old trails and now they have to stop the traffic each time this one makes his nightly commute.

Some wild animals actually seem to do better living near humans than they did in their natural habitats. City pigeons are descendants of wild rock doves that nest along rugged coastlines. To these feral pigeons, high-rise buildings are cliffs and they feed well on the food scraps people leave as litter. Truly wild rock doves have become rare, while feral pigeons thrive all over the world. In places, the predators that hunt them have made the move to urban life too. Peregrine falcons also make their nests on tall buildings. In central London, there is a pair living on one of the towers of Battersea power station. While many people welcome the sight of these rare and beautiful birds, their prey – pigeons (and other natural survivors like rats, which live in their millions in cities across the world) – are just seen as pests. But, make no mistake, if people disappeared, these and all the other "urban wildlife" would be among the first to take over.

It doesn't take much to rewild an urban wasteland or a deserted city. It just needs to be left alone with a supply of animals, plants, fungi and bacteria nearby that can move into the vacant spaces. Life can come back even when habitats have been destroyed completely. This is what happened at the volcanic island of Krakatoa.

2 Natural disasters and extinction events

Krakatoa – back from nothing!

August 1883. An island in the Sunda Strait between Java and Sumatra in what is now called Indonesia.

The captain of a steamship chugging past reports clouds of ash billowing out from the island's mountain top, and deep rumbling and explosive noises that sound like gun shots. This is nothing all that unusual. The volcano has been active off and on like this for years.

But no one is quite prepared for what happens on 29 August.
They couldn't have been. Never in recorded history has a
volcano exploded with such force. The island blows itself
sky high. Millions of tons of ash and rocks are blasted into
the atmosphere. The blast and the giant tsunami waves
that follow kill 37,000 people and wipe 160 coastal villages
in nearby Java and Sumatra off the map. The explosion is
loud enough to be heard in Alice Springs in Australia 3,600
kilometres away. The ash thrown up into the atmosphere
makes sunsets all over the world extra red for more than a
year afterwards.

Surely nothing could survive.

Two thirds of Krakatoa island had been blown away or fallen into the sea, but some fragments remained. The largest, Rakata, with 800-metre-high cliffs on the side facing the blast site, was the remaining fragment of the volcano's cone. It and the nearby islands of Sertung and Panjang were smothered tens of metres deep with red-hot ash that incinerated everything it touched. All life was killed. But not for long.

When the ash clouds cleared, birds were seen flying over the islands. Some landed. Fallen trees and bits of plants washed up on the barren coastlines. Some of this vegetation contained seeds, and these seeds grew. Only 35 years after the explosion, Rakata was covered in trees. A decade later, the treetops had covered most of the island with a **rainforest canopy** – a regrown forest like this is called a "secondary forest". Similar things were happening on Sertung and Panjang. There was also now another island that had appeared from the sea: Anak Krakatoa, which means "Child of Krakatoa", a new volcano that was washed back under the water three times until it finally surfaced for good in 1930.

This is a timeline of what happened next. It involves a lot of extinctions as plants and animals arrived, survived for a while, then were wiped out by more eruptions. Anak Krakatau was – and still is – a *very* active volcano.

1930 For six months, Anak Krakatau is too hot and too active for boats to land. When they do get ashore, scientists find one beetle on the ash, insect-like springtails in floating plants by the shore, several ants, a small leaf-mining moth (its larvae burrow through leaves), one mosquito and three types of spiders. These have been blown in by the wind.

1932 Six types of plant found. Some of the seeds in the debris of sticks on the beaches are sprouting. Some birds called "thick-knees" have flown in from Java or Sumatra and are picking through the ash, looking for insects and spiders to eat.

1930s More birds have arrived, including three owls which are preying on the other birds that are living on the island.

1939 The growing volcano erupts fully, smothering the whole area with ash again. There are more eruptions over the next few years but no one visits.

coconut palm

oriental thick-knee

1947 The captain of a passing ship reports that grasslands have taken hold, along with casuarina trees. Some of these are up to three metres tall. Casuarina is a "pioneer" plant that, along with coconut palms, grows on beaches all around the tropics. "Pioneer" means it's one of the first plants to establish itself.

1952 Another eruption. Lots more birds have arrived, including a white-bellied fish eagle, which is seen flying around after the eruption stops.

1953 Anak Krakatau erupts again, covering the whole island with ash that kills everything off.

1958 Another eruption. A biologist looking through binoculars from his boat reports seeing casuarina trees and grassland growing on the land that is not covered in ash.

1971 Trees and shrubs have grown back. Many are killed in yet another eruption in 1972.

1982 Scientists report a "continuous rain of airborne **arthropods**". Insects and spiders keep falling from the sky. There are spiders, beetles, wasps, ants and large numbers of crickets on the patches that are still bare ash. Following the insects are insect-eating birds, like swifts and grey wagtails. There are also several types of bat, including fruit bats which, along with birds like emerald doves, are spreading the seeds of fig trees in their droppings. On the beaches, monitor lizards have been seen. It is thought that these feed on shore crabs and the eggs of green turtles which have started to nest.

1992 The remaining grassland is growing over with fig trees. There are several types of birds, but most of the grassland types have gone extinct or moved on. The top predator is now the peregrine falcon and this seems to have driven off another smaller type of falcon, the oriental hobby, which until recently had been hunting the smaller birds. Brown rats and closely-related Malayan field rats have arrived. They might have floated in on rafts of vegetation or have been introduced accidentally when boats landed on the island. Amongst their varied diet are the eggs and young of ground-nesting birds. The rats are preyed on by reticulated pythons. These can grow up to six metres long. On Rakata, there are also 30-centimetre-long Tokay geckoes, paradise tree snakes which can glide from tree to tree, and various types of frogs.

reticulated python

The peregrine falcon is the top predator.

2018 Rakata is covered with secondary rainforest, much of it over 20 metres tall. There are 200 species of plants, 70 types of vertebrates (backboned animals like birds, rats and snakes) and thousands of invertebrates (insects, spiders and crustaceans like crabs). Anak Krakatau has fewer species because of the frequent volcanic eruptions. The forest on these islands will never have the same **biodiversity** as the rainforest on the mainland. The islands are tiny. There simply is not enough food for a leopard or an elephant to survive, even if one managed to swim there. Even so, considering the disaster that happened, the bounce-back of life has been astounding, a true case of nature fighting back.

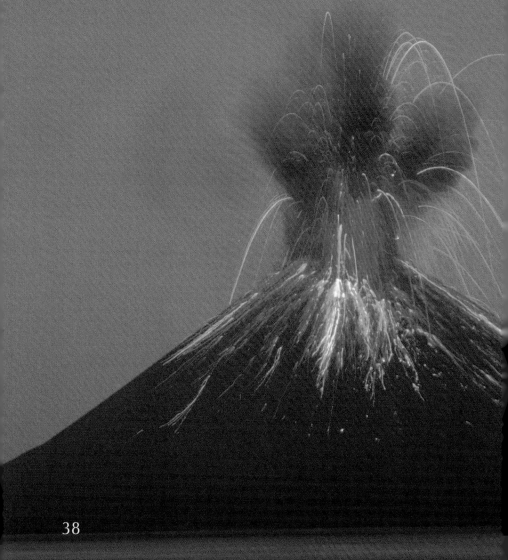

But, Anak Krakatau is one of the most active volcanoes in the world. It has been growing 6.8 metres taller every year and by the end of 2018 the volcano's cone is 310 metres high. It erupts again. The western two-thirds of the island collapse into the sea, and much of what is left is smothered with ash. There are more eruptions in 2020.

Scientists are certain that life will come back to Anak Krakatau. The process of ecological succession will repeat again. As before, many of the species will not last long but will die out as their food source changes or the volcano erupts again, as it certainly will.

Extinction events

Sixty-six million years ago, a comet hit Earth and wiped out nearly 80% of all living species, including the dinosaurs on the land, the plesiosaurs in the oceans and the pterosaurs in the sky. There was so much dust hanging in the atmosphere for years afterwards that most plants did not have enough sunlight to grow.

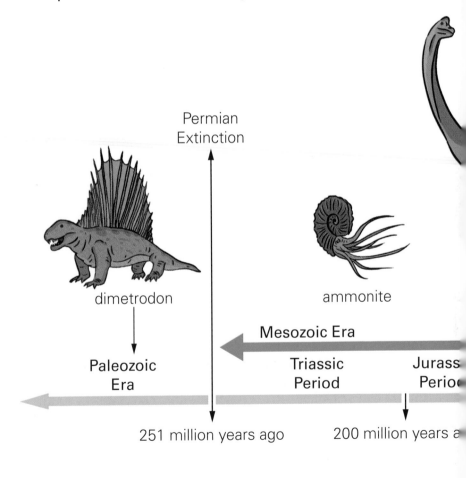

Permian
Extinction

dimetrodon

ammonite

Mesozoic Era

Paleozoic
Era

Triassic
Period

Jurass
Perio

251 million years ago

200 million years a

The exceptions were some types of fern which could cope with the low light levels and so became very successful. (A similar thing happened for a while at Krakatoa.) With less vegetation to eat, only small animals survived: insects, a few mammals, birds, and reptiles like lizards and tortoises. The oceans were not affected as badly as the land though. In addition to the plesiosaurs, a few families like the ammonites (think of squid with shells) became extinct.

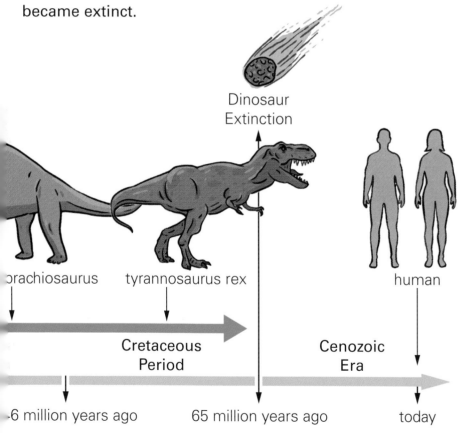

Dinosaur Extinction

brachiosaurus   tyrannosaurus rex   human

Cretaceous
Period

Cenozoic
Era

-6 million years ago   65 million years ago   today

What had the species that went extinct done wrong?

Nothing: it was just that their lifestyles, diet and preferred habitat didn't fit with the changes that suddenly happened. When life came back, it was different to before. There were different habitats with different species evolving to survive in them, like snakes, whales, horses, elephants, monkeys and (eventually) human beings. People recognisable as looking like us have only been around for about 200,000 years. Compare this with the age of our planet (4.5 billion years) and the 500 million years that complex life like molluscs (snails and octopi) and vertebrates (animals with backbones) have lived on it. Our species is a really recent addition to life on Earth.

The comet impact that wiped out the dinosaurs was only one of many extinction events that have affected the planet. The most destructive of these happened 250 million years ago when all the landmasses were clumped together into one gigantic continent and the climate became much drier and hotter. This climate change killed off 90% of all forms of life. Before then, mammal-like reptiles had been among the most successful large land animals. Afterwards, it was another group of reptiles that came to dominate Earth. The dinosaurs.

The next extinction event

It has been said that the human race is causing the next extinction event right now. Species of animals and plants are going extinct more often than at any time since the end of the dinosaurs. In just the last century, Earth has lost large mammals like the thylacine "Tasmanian wolf" (actually a marsupial more closely related to a kangaroo), the Yangtse river dolphin and the Balinese tiger. Many types of birds, reptiles, fish and amphibians have also disappeared, as well as countless types of insects and plants that have gone extinct, more or less unnoticed.

In time, some of the species that are left will evolve into different species to fill the gaps. But evolution takes millions of years. Besides, this extinction event need not happen. Humans are the most intelligent life form to have developed on this planet. We are clever enough to keep the animals and plants we already have – *if* we act before it is too late.

the now-extinct thylacine

3 Human threats to nature

These can be summed up with the letters HIPPO, which stand for **H**abitat, **Invasive species**, **P**opulation, **P**ollution and **O**ver-harvesting.

Habitats are being destroyed. For example, humans are cutting down the rainforest and clearing land for farming or to build cities.

Invasive species like rats take over (invade) habitats and drive out or kill off the original inhabitants.

Population. The number of people in the world is huge and still growing. There are nearly eight billion (8,000,000,000) people alive today, twice as many as there were 50 years ago. They all need water and food, not to mention fuel and electricity for transport and communications like TV and the internet.

Pollution. Using all those resources makes millions of tons of waste. Burning fossil fuels, such as oil and natural gas, makes more carbon dioxide than plants can absorb and this is leading to global warming and climate change.

Over-harvesting. We humans are also over-harvesting many of the living things on our planet. For example: we catch more fish in the oceans than can replenish themselves and we cut down trees in the forests faster than new ones can grow and take their place.

Natural survivors

Some plants and animals are natural survivors, such as the pests that do so well in our cities. Wherever there is new habitat – like a deserted city or an island without predators – these are usually the first to move in.

The problem can be that sometimes they take over. They crowd the original inhabitants out of their habitat; they eat their food or they eat them.

This is what invasive species have in common:

- They can survive on all sorts of food, often what we throw away as waste. Animals that feed on many things are called "generalists". When one supply of food runs out, there is usually something else they can eat.

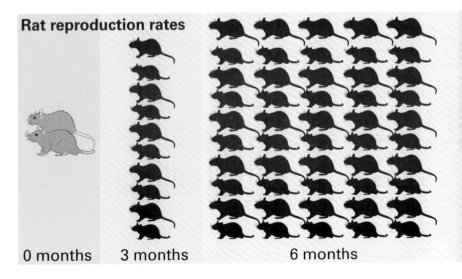

Rat reproduction rates

0 months   3 months   6 months

- They are usually small, there are lots of them and they reproduce and grow up quickly. Huge numbers are born to make up for the many that are killed. A rat can have six litters of around ten young each year, and each rat is ready to breed at nine weeks old. It's estimated that one pair of rats can produce around 1,200 descendants in one year. By then, the original pair would be great-great-great-great-grandparents to the newest born.

- They live, sleep and breed in places that are hard for humans to get to. Rats often live in sewers underground. Pigeons nest on ledges on tall buildings. Cockroaches breed between our walls and under our floors.

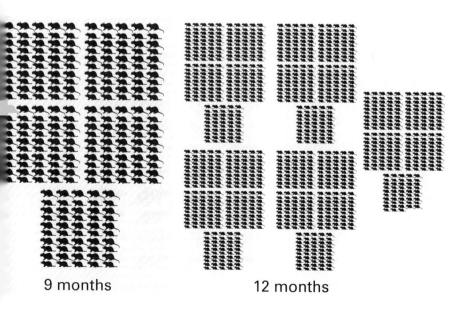

9 months   12 months

There are also pests in the seas, for example, long-spined sea urchins which swarm over kelp seaweed (we will come across these later) and the crown-of-thorns starfish which are destroying the coral of Australia's Great Barrier Reef. Both eat greedily and breed quickly, with few or no natural predators to keep their numbers down.

There are plant pests too. Japanese knotweed was "introduced" to Britain in the 19th century as gardeners admired its flowers and liked the way it grew so quickly. But there are no herbivorous animals that eat it, so it grows unchecked.

The opposite to these survivors that can live almost anywhere and on a wide variety of foods are species that are called "specialists". These usually have a diet that is limited to just a few things and they reproduce slowly. Specialists are easily driven to extinction. Take, for instance, a giant panda: human-sized, it eats just one or two types of bamboo and breeds – if it can find a mate – only every three to four years. Unlike rats, pigeons or even foxes, there is no such thing as an urban panda, and unlike them, pandas are endangered. With our growing human population squeezing wildlife into smaller and more separated habitats, it's the specialists that die out first. True, nature fights back, but sometimes humans have to take action if it is not just going to be the invasive species, nature's natural survivors, that are left.

4 People helping the natural world

Gorongosa – living with wild nature

Mozambique. South East Africa. 1992.

After a civil war raged through the country, the people were starving. So, they ate any large wild mammals that they could find. The soldiers on both sides were armed with automatic rifles and the meat from one elephant would feed a lot of troops, not to mention the money they could earn by cutting off and selling the precious tusks for ivory. An army needs a lot of food. The elephants were wiped out. So were zebras and antelopes like nyalas and waterbucks, as well as the animals that preyed on them. Almost all were killed, except for a lucky few that had remained hidden or out of range of the soldiers' guns.

When the war ended, the armies moved on, leaving a burnt land with little wildlife and a lot of starving people.

In Gorongosa, what happened next was different from the other places affected. The people who had survived the war got on with their lives. They grew their crops. Some of the wild animals came back and people hunted them because they still needed food. But there was little to eat, and life was about surviving until the next meal, nothing more. It was clear a plan had to be made or Gorongosa would go the way of so many war-torn areas, empty of trees and wildlife, full of starving people.

When the government said they wanted to keep Gorongosa as a national park, not everyone was pleased. "Humans need saving, not wildlife," many people said. "Places like Gorongosa may be beautiful, but they do not keep us fed."

Others thought that people can live alongside wild nature and that growing back the forest and savanna bush country would actually make life for all better than before. The most important part of the plan has been to get everyone involved at every stage. Most of these stages do not even involve conserving natural habitats or the wild animals in them. They are as follows:

- Spending money on hospitals and education, particularly for girls who in the past have had little schooling. Better educated people know how to improve their lives and understand why it is important to look after the area.

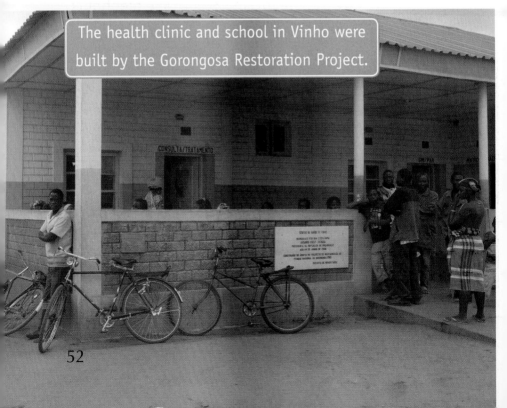

The health clinic and school in Vinho were built by the Gorongosa Restoration Project.

- Stopping all hunting in the central zone of Gorongosa. The land needs to regenerate. Hopefully, some animals will find their way back naturally. Some, like elephants, are being reintroduced into the national park from South Africa where there are lots of them. Local people, women especially, are employed as park guards to protect the wildlife, mainly by removing the wire noose snares that poachers set to trap antelopes and other mammals.

- Making a "buffer zone" around the central area where some hunting for food and felling of trees for timber is allowed. People can farm some of the land there. Many are growing coffee on the higher, wetter hillsides. This brings money in.

The project has been going since 2004. Habitats are growing back and the number of wild animals is steadily rising. Waterbucks are doing especially well. So are painted wolves which were reintroduced to the park in 2018. The wildlife is not as numerous as it was before the war, but it will be in time. Perhaps, most importantly, the people in the area have become better educated and wealthier. They live alongside the wild animals and do not hunt them for food anymore. They no longer need to.

The project is now being expanded. Soon it will join up a string of nature reserves, each with slightly different habitats, stretching 250 kilometres all the way from Gorongosa in the hills to the sea.

In Gorongosa and many other places around the world, people have been actively involved in saving wild nature, but sometimes, it is just a case of not doing something – like not overhunting. Allowing one or two **keystone species** *to come back can rebalance a whole ecosystem.*

painted wolves

Kelp forests – saved by sea otters

The kelp forest off the Californian coast has been lucky. It has been saved by sea otters.

Kelp is a fast-growing brown seaweed that anchors itself on to the seabed and grows upwards towards the light. Kelp is only found in a few areas of the world, like off the western coast of North America where the water is cold, clear and shallow enough for sunlight to reach the bottom. Here, kelp grows into thick floating forests up to 20 metres tall.

Beaufort Sea

Bering Sea

Davis Strait

U.S.A.

PACIFIC OCEAN

CANADA

Sea kelp forest

UNITED STATES OF AMERICA

MEXICO

Along with coral reefs, kelp forests are one of the most biodiverse ecosystems in the oceans. Sea ferns trap nutrient particles on fine hairs. Top shells (marine snails) graze on algae on the kelp leaves. Cuttlefish and black bream hunt smaller fish, and seals hunt them. Fish and squid lay their eggs in the calm water beneath the forest canopy.

Kelp is useful to humans who can use it to make biodegradable plastic packaging that rots away into the soil after it has been thrown away. Kelp forests lock in carbon dioxide gas and this helps reduce global warming. The forests also absorb the energy in the ocean's waves and protect coasts against storms. What's more, they provide a nursery where many fish that we catch for food grow up.

But, around the world, kelp forests are being destroyed by long-spined sea urchins. A combination of the seas warming and a virus that has killed off the starfish that eat these sea urchins has made their numbers soar. In places, up to a hundred sea urchins swarm on every square metre. They eat their way through the kelp stems, then use their hard mouth parts to scrape away creatures such as barnacles and cold-water corals off the rocks that they live on. When they have run out of food, long-spined sea urchins can shut down their body processes for up to 50 years and start feeding again when conditions change. They have turned areas of the seabed around Japan and Tasmania into "urchin barrens", sea deserts where little else survives.

But, off the coast of California and British Columbia to the north, help is at hand. Sea otters. These animals spend most of their lives in the water and only rarely come to land. They live in family groups called "rafts" amongst the kelp, wrapping it around their tails and bodies to stay anchored while they sleep. Sea otters eat shellfish, like clams, and also sea urchins. The spikes don't bother them. The otters use their flipper-like feet to push themselves down to the sea bottom, pick up the urchins and bring them to the surface where they float on their backs and feed on them. They have developed the knack of turning

the shells over with their hand-flippers and using their powerful jaws to crunch into the less well-defended underparts to get at the soft flesh inside.

The result is that where there are sea otters, there is kelp forest. But it's lucky there are still sea otters at all as they were nearly hunted to extinction for their thick fur, which used to be highly prized for hats and coats. By 1911, there were only 2,000 sea otters left in the world. Now there are around 125,000. Sea otters have been called a keystone species. Protecting them saves the whole kelp forest ecosystem.

Did you know?

People have long known that shipwrecks, like those at Chuuk lagoon, attract marine life and provide surfaces for coral reefs to grow on. In many places, ships have been sunk on purpose to make artificial reefs. So have concrete blocks. This is because concrete has tiny holes where coral polyps can take hold. In the Caribbean Sea, 3-D-printed, hand-sized concrete stars have been "seeded" with polyps and wedged into damaged reefs. Elkhorn coral, set down like this near to the island of Curaçao, has been found not just to have grown but to be breeding only four years later.

Projects like this can rebuild reefs but they can't yet deal with the main threat to coral, which is global warming. Warmer seawater is slightly acidic and this can kill coral polyps in reefs, leaving just their white stony casings. The effect is called "coral bleaching" and, although some types of coral can survive in the warmer water, the only way to preserve reefs around the world in the long term is to tackle climate change.

Preserving keystone species like sea otters can save whole ecosystems. Sometimes, the creatures to save seem to go against logic, like saving top predators when you want more animals or saving an animal that cuts down trees when preserving trees is one of the best ways to stop man-made climate change.

Introducing beavers and wolves – and preventing floods

Beavers are what scientists call "**ecosystem engineers**". They change their habitat to make it a better place for them to live. They use their strong incisor teeth to gnaw down riverside trees to build dams across rivers and to eat the nutritious layer underneath the trees' bark. But trees absorb carbon dioxide and reducing carbon dioxide reduces global warming. Surely introducing an animal that kills trees goes against this?

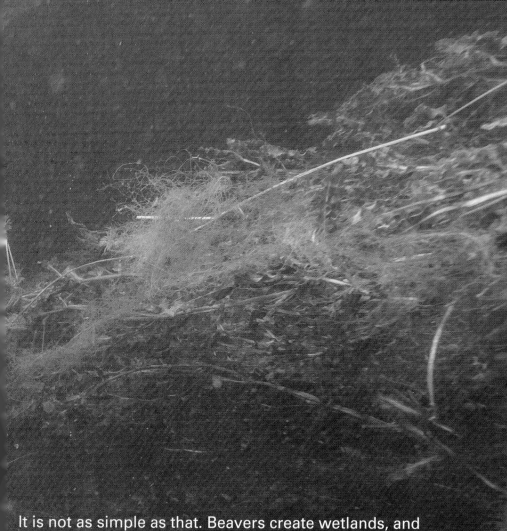

It is not as simple as that. Beavers create wetlands, and
wetlands also absorb carbon dioxide. Water-loving plants
like lilies and cattails thrive in the flooded areas behind
their dams. These provide food for the beavers (who
eat their roots) and habitat for a wide variety of species
like water voles, otters and dragonflies. Having beavers
around increases the biodiversity of an area.

Beaver dams can also be good news for people. With our climate changing, many areas are suffering worse storms than ever before. Beaver dams always leak slightly and can lessen the effects of the floods by storing water upstream and letting it out slowly. If it looks like their dam is going to be washed away, the beavers that made it will remove some branches for a while to allow water to flow through. If the dam breaks completely, they will rebuild it. In effect, they provide flood defences and they maintain them for free. Having beaver dams can be good for people and for wildlife during dry weather too. As their dams always leak some water, in times of drought, the river downstream keeps flowing.

This is why beavers are being protected in river habitats across Europe. In Britain, wild beavers were hunted to extinction for their fur during the 16th century. Now, some have been taken out of the wild in Norway where they are common and reintroduced into rivers from Devon and Kent in the south of England up to north-west Scotland. The animals are first put into large enclosures to get used to the change in scenery and for vets to check they are healthy before they are released. At present, there are far more landowners wanting beavers than there are beavers available to put into the rivers. It seems everyone wants these animals which can make flood defences for free.

So where do wolves come in? Can we save beavers by saving wolves?

That wouldn't be the first thing you would think wolves would do – as wolves eat beavers. But here is the reason why.

Yellowstone National Park in the USA is a vast area of wilderness, centred on volcanic geysers and bubbling hot springs. In the 1990s, there were hardly any wolves and even fewer beavers. The place was overrun with large deer called elk, and young trees could not grow as the deer nibbled the new shoots. The park's main predators back then were coyotes. These small wolf-relatives are too puny to bring down an elk. Something had to be done. Yellowstone was losing wolves and beavers, mammals that it was famous for. The solution: add more wolves. But wolves hunt and kill other animals. Wasn't a wolf introduction going to ruin what the national park was there for – nature conservation?

Some wolves were brought from nearby Canada, and over time the food web changed. A food web is the combination of all the food chains in an ecosystem. Before the wolf reintroduction, one of these food chains was *elks eat leaves from young trees.* Another was *coyotes eat sage grouse – and sage grouse eat sage brush leaves.*

YELLOWSTONE
NATIONAL
PARK

47

Old Faithful

Museum

After the wolf introduction, wolves hunted the elks and so their numbers went down. Also, just as important, the elks were scared of wolves, so they did not stand around eating all the young trees. Added to that, the wolves drove off or killed coyotes if they got a chance.

The result: fewer coyotes, fewer elks and many more ground-nesting birds like sage grouse. Trees grew back, especially along the riversides. Beaver numbers went up. Wetlands got bigger and so did the biodiversity.

As of 2020, there were around 90 wolves in eight packs in Yellowstone. There have been problems though. Some local ranchers outside the national park have complained that wolves have preyed on their cattle and want to be allowed to shoot them. Wolf numbers are now increasing over much of Europe, as more people live in cities and areas of countryside are rewilding. Britain has no wolves anymore. They were hunted to extinction in the 18th century. But the Scottish Highlands, in particular, have so many deer that the forest there can't regenerate. Reintroducing wolves there is a plan that might one day sort this problem out.

5 Nature fights back

Wild nature comes back even when a place has been blasted clean or poisoned. But there are conditions.

- There have to be species nearby that can move in.

- There has to be time – and the more time, the more biodiverse a place can become.

- The conditions that damaged or destroyed the life there in the first place must have stopped or at least greatly lessened.

The nature that returns to an area may not be the same as it was before. There may be a different mix of plants and animals. Ecosystems are not stable. Food webs change as living things jostle for survival.

Humans can live with life on Earth because we are part of nature too. Like beavers, coral and elephants in the African bush, we are ecosystem engineers, only our species can change things on a global scale. We can live our lives more sustainably, limit the spread of invasive species and stop polluting our planet. We can give fragile habitats the help they need to recover.

Everyone can do this. We can waste less and recycle more. We can use renewable forms of energy and get around without using as much fossil fuel, as carbon dioxide pollution leads to global warming and climate change.

At home, we can rewild our gardens by putting in a pond, planting trees or leaving a lawn to grow long with wildflowers whose nectar insects can feed on. Even growing plants (preferably native ones) in a pot on a window ledge will create a micro-habitat. It is important to remember that the creatures at the bottom of all food chains are the most important. That pot of soil will swarm with bacteria, fungi and tiny invertebrates feeding on dead plant matter, converting it into nutrients that the plant needs to grow. Some of these "decomposers" will be large enough to see, like worms and woodlice. There may be predators too, such as tiny spiders or centipedes that wriggle through the earth. There will be a whole ecosystem in miniature and, given a chance, like a bit of spilt soil or a dead leaf falling on to a window ledge, that tiny patch of wilderness will spread.

One thing is for certain: life will find a way.

Glossary

algae simple plants that live in water and do not flower

arthropods animals with segmented bodies and many legs like insects, spiders and springtails

biodiversity the variety of living things

contamination poison or radioactivity that stays in a place – such as in the soil

ecological succession the way that species take over from each other as ecosystems change

ecosystems all the connected living things – plants, animals, fungi and so on – in their environment

ecosystem engineers species that change their habitat, usually to make it a better place for them to live in

extinctions when species are wiped out completely, never to come back

extinction events disasters that make many creatures go extinct at the same time

habitats places where living things live

invasive species animals or plants from somewhere else that move in and change ecosystems; because invasive species do not usually have predators in their new home, they often take over and drive local species towards extinction

keystone species a species that is critically important for an ecosystem

nuclear power station a "factory" that generates electricity by splitting the atoms of uranium metal

nutrients substances that provide material for growth and life

polyps jellyfish-like animals which make up coral; they build up rocky casings around their bodies which join together to make coral reefs

rainforest canopy when the treetops form a continuous layer that shades the ground

rewilding restoring areas of land or sea to their natural uncultivated state

species a group or type of living things that can breed together, for example tigers or willow trees

temperate with mild temperatures

Rewilding

1. Damaged habitats

2. Natural disasters and extinction events

3. Human threats to nature

4. People helping the natural world

5. Nature fights back

6. What can we do?

 Ideas for reading

Written by Gill Matthews
Lecturer and Primary Literacy Consultant

Reading objectives:

- read books that are structured in different ways and read for a range of purposes
- check the book makes sense to them, discussing their understanding and exploring the meaning of words in context
- summarise the main ideas drawn from more than one paragraph, identifying key details that support the main ideas
- retrieve, record and present information from non-fiction

Spoken language objectives:

- use spoken language to develop understanding through speculating, hypothesising, imagining and exploring ideas
- participate in discussion, presentations, performances, role play/ improvisations and debates

Curriculum links: Geography – Human and physical geography; Science – Living things and their habitats

Interest words: habitat, invasive species, population, pollution, over-harvesting

Build a context for reading

- Look at the front cover and read the title. What do children think this book is about? What kind of book is it?
- Read the blurb. Check children's understanding of rewilding.
- Discuss the three examples of rewilding given in the blurb. Encourage children to speculate why these events might take place.

Understand and apply reading strategies

- Read pp2–5. Encourage children to make links between the text and the photos, speculating on what is happening in each image.
- Focus on the contents page. Ask children to choose a chapter to read from Chapters 1–4. They can read it, noting down the main points. They can then present a summary to the rest of the group.